CHILDREN'S LIBRARY

Palo Alto City Library

The individual borrower is responsible for all library material borrowed on his or her card.

Charges as determined by the CITY OF PALO ALTO will be assessed for each overdue item.

Damaged or non-returned property will be billed to the individual borrower by the CITY OF PALO ALTO.

I'm going to New York to visit the Queen

by Patty Wolcott
illustrated by Blair Drawson

♠Addison-Wesley

*"To all children
who are learning to read"*

Addisonian Press titles by Patty Wolcott
Beware of a Very Hungry Fox
The Cake Story
The Forest Fire
I'm Going to New York to Visit the Queen
The Marvelous Mud Washing Machine
My Shadow and I
Pickle Pickle Pickle Juice
Super Sam and the Salad Garden
Tunafish Sandwiches
Where Did That Naughty Little Hamster Go?

 **An Addisonian Press Book**

Library of Congress Cataloging in Publication Data
Wolcott, Patty.
    I'm going to New York to visit the Queen.
    SUMMARY: Two children walk through the streets of
New York and visit the ship, Queen Elizabeth II.
    "An Addisonian Press book."
    [1. Queen Elizabeth 2 (Ship)—Fiction]
I. Drawson, Blair, illus.   II. Title.
PZ7.W8185Im   [E]   74-730
ISBN 0-201-14248-1

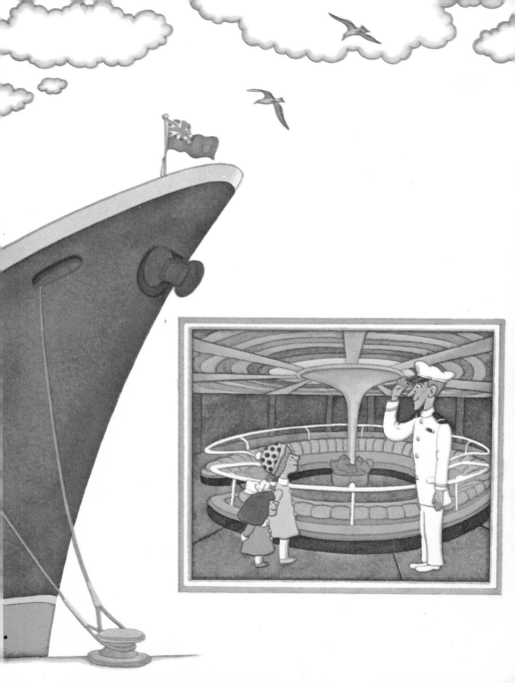

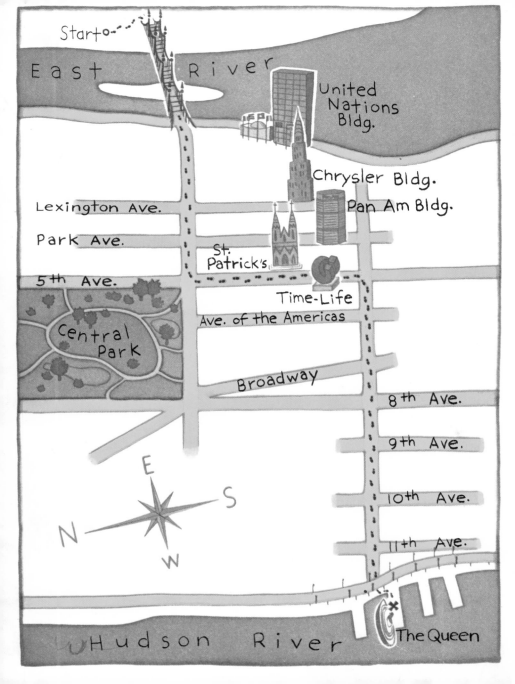